To
JANE O'CONNOR:
This
is
yours,
all
yours.

Library of Congress Cataloging-in-Publication Data
Heller, Ruth, 1924–
Mine, all mine : a book about pronouns / written and illustrated
by Ruth Heller. p. cm.
Summary: Introduces various types of pronouns, explains how and
when to use them, and provides whimsical glimpses of what our
language would be without them.
1. English language—Pronoun—Juvenile literature.
[1. English language—Pronoun.] I. Title.
PE1261.H394
1997 428.2—dc21 97-10051 CIP AC

ISBN 0-448-41606-9
C D E F G H I J

Mine, All Mine

A Book About Pronouns

Written and illustrated by
RUTH HELLER

Publishers GROSSET & DUNLAP · New York

PRONOUNS take
the place of nouns...

so we don't have to say...

"Mike said
Mike walked
Mike's dogs
today.

Mike
walked
Mike's
dogs
a long,
long way."

How
boring...

what we say would be
without the PRONOUNS
his and **he**!

King Cole
would
call for
King Cole's
pipe.
King Cole
would
call for
King Cole's
bowl
and
King Cole's
fiddlers
three.

On and on...
it makes me yawn.
It's awkward and wordy.
The rhythm is gone.

And so...
hooray, hip hip hooray,
for
PERSONAL PRONOUNS
you, **it**, **them**, **they**,
for
us and **we**
and
I and **me**,
for
him and **her**
and
he and **she**.

These
are the most common
PRONOUNS
we use,
but
sometimes it's tricky
to know
which to choose.

Which should it be...the king
is
him
or
the king
is
he?

Reverse
the sentence
and
you'll see.

He
is the
king...
so
the king
is
he.

Are these for **he** and **I**, or are they for **him** and **me**?
Try each PRONOUN separately.
They aren't for I. They are for **me**.

They are for
him,
and not for
he...

so
they're
for **him**
and
me.

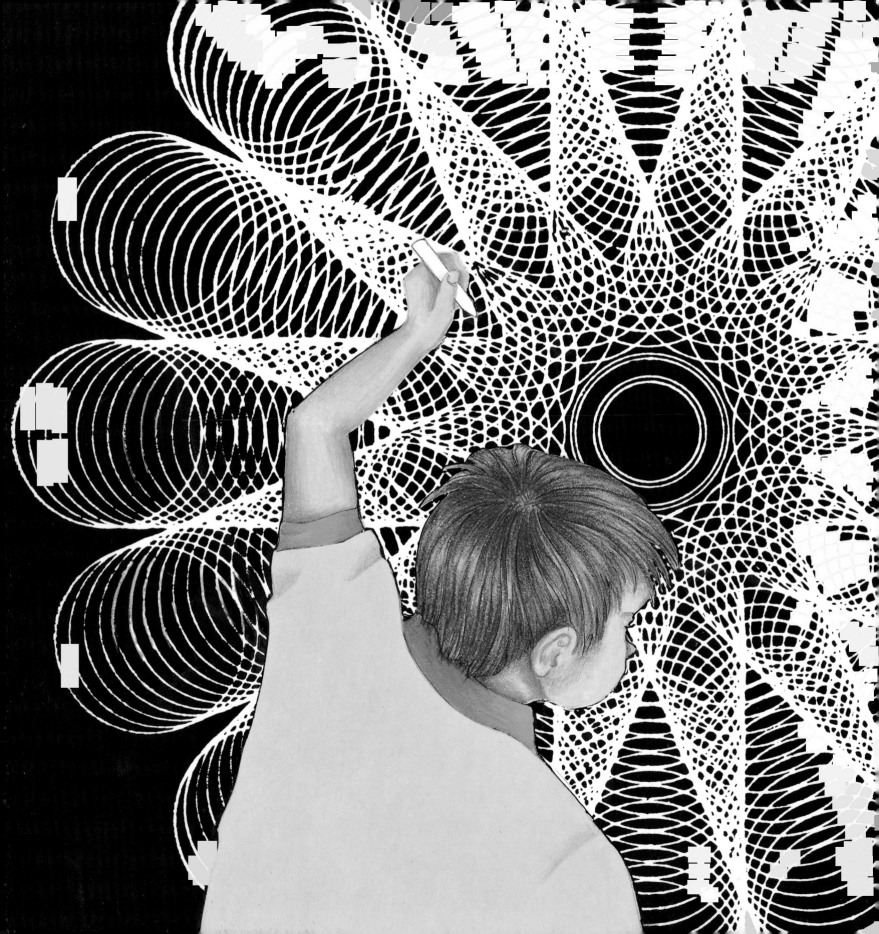

Does he draw better than **her**, or does he draw better than **she**?

The missing word is "draws."

He draws better than **she** draws, so he draws better than **she**.

We brag...so **we** (not us) Americans brag...

of fifty stars upon our flag.

But...
she
told
us,
so
she told
us boys,
that
we were
making
too much
noise.

Some PERSONAL PRONOUNS are also
POSSESSIVE.
All these presents are
impressive.

They are **mine**. They are all **mine**. How handsomely **their** ribbons shine.

If... I said,

"Everyone stood on **his** head," I'd be correct but not quite fair, because there are some females there.

His or **her** head is what I really...

should
have
said.

DEMONSTRATIVE PRONOUNS make it clear.

Those
are
far.

These
are
near.

They
point out
decisively.

This is she, and that...

is he.

INDEFINITE
PRONOUNS
are
vague
instead.

Many
behind...

few
ahead.

Someone's
sleeping
in
my
bed.

REFLEXIVE PRONOUNS end in "self."
This messy elf just helped
himself.

REFLEXIVE PRONOUNS
are
INTENSIVE
when they emphasize or stress.

He **himself** made this mess. He made this mess **himself**
He is a messy elf.

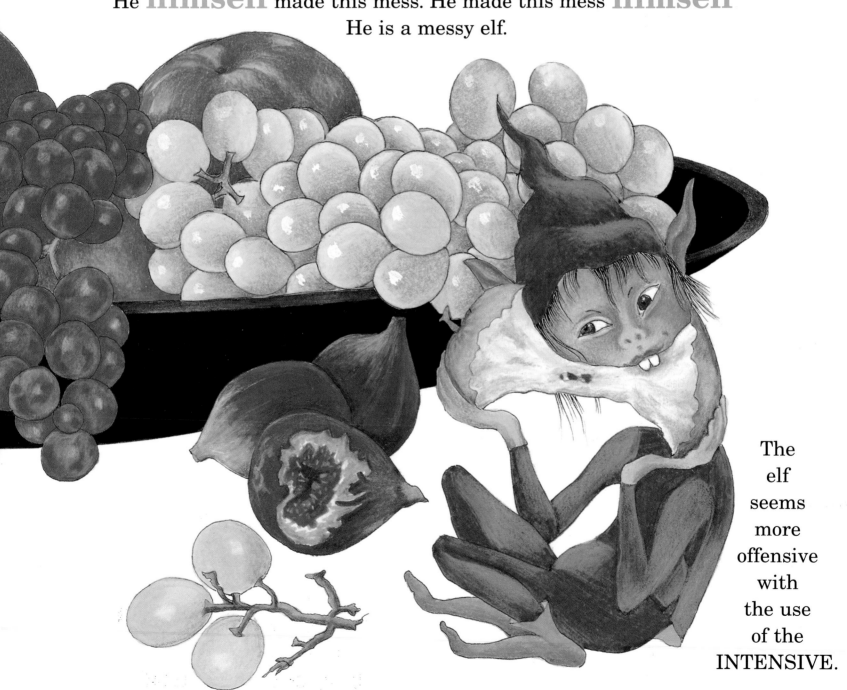

The
elf
seems
more
offensive
with
the use
of the
INTENSIVE.

REFLEXIVE
plurals
end
in
"selves."

The
other elves
amused
themselves.

PRONOUNS
can ask
questions,
too.

INTERROGATIVE
PRONOUNS
do.

Who

had a nose
that
grew and grew?

RELATIVE PRONOUNS
make a
connection.

Here
is
Narcissus,
who
loved
his
reflection.

These three are all winners.

There's no way you can lose.

You
will
be
a
champion
whichever
one
you
choose.

Whichever's
a
RELATIVE
PRONOUN,
too.

When
should
you
say
whom,
and
when...

should you say
who?

Whom
is the one to
whom
something is done,
and
who
is the one
who
does it.

She is the one
who
was dressed in red
to
whom
the carnivorous
grandmother said,
"The better
to eat you
with,
my dear."

PRONOUNS
make our language flow.
These are
the
different kinds to know:

PERSONAL and POSSESSIVE
I   me   my   mine
you   your   yours
he   him   his
she   her   hers
it   its
we   us   our   ours
they   them   their   theirs

DEMONSTRATIVE
this   that   these   those

RELATIVE
that   which   who   whom   whose
whoever   whomever   whatever   whichever

INTERROGATIVE
what   which   who   whom   whose

INDEFINITE

all	everything	none
another	few	no one
any	fewer	nothing
anybody	fewest	one
anyone	little	other
anything	many	others
both	more	several
each	most	some
either	much	somebody
everybody	neither	someone
everyone	nobody	something

REFLEXIVE and INTENSIVE

myself   yourself   himself   herself

oneself   itself

ourselves   yourselves   themselves

You will never
be
outclassed
if you put
"**I**"
or
"**me**"
last.

Say,
"he and **I**"
or
"him and **me**"
not
"me and him"
or
"I and he."